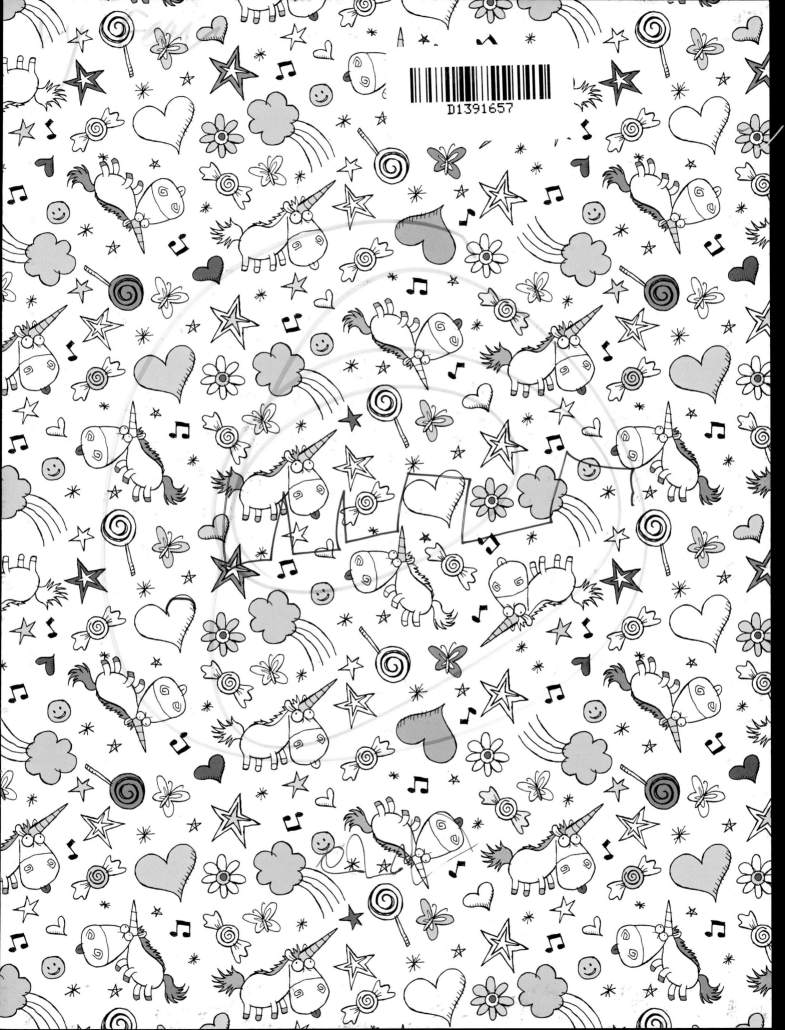

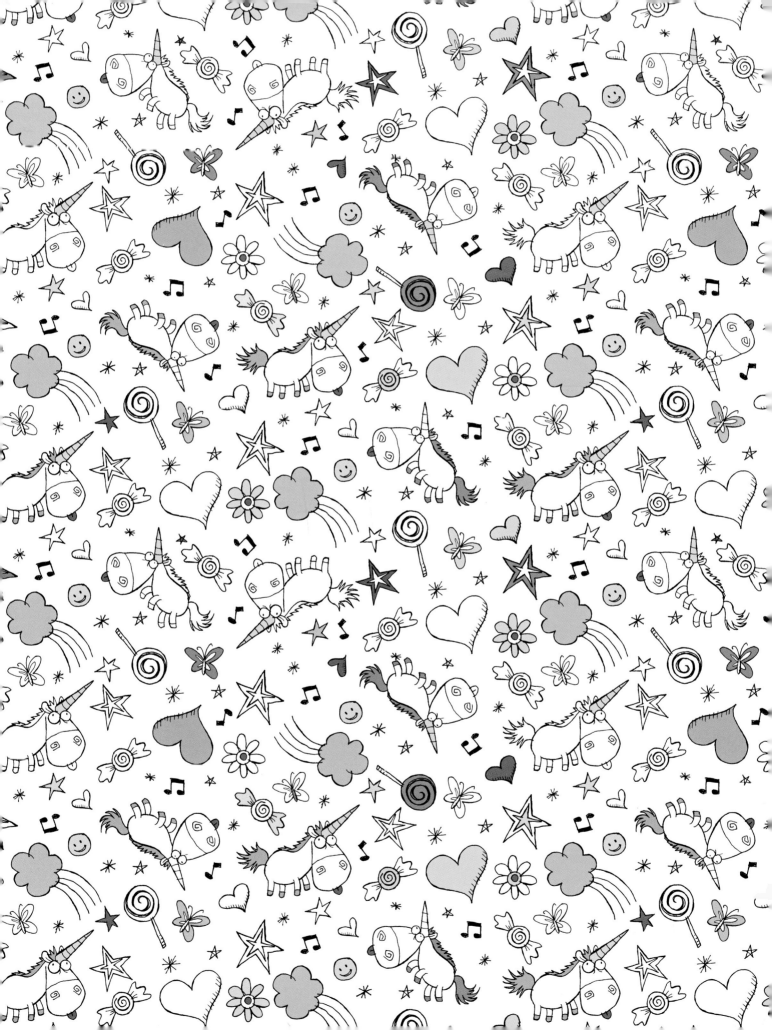

ILLUMINATION PRESENTS
DESPICABLE ME 3™

THE GREAT UNICORN QUEST

DESPICABLE ME 3: THE GREAT UNICORN QUEST

A CENTUM BOOK 9781911461494

PUBLISHED IN GREAT BRITAIN BY CENTUM BOOKS LTD

THIS EDITION PUBLISHED 2017

© 2017 UNIVERSAL STUDIOS.

1 3 5 7 9 10 8 6 4 2

CENTUM BOOKS LTD, 20 DEVON SQUARE, NEWTON ABBOT, DEVON, TQ12 2HR, UK

BOOKS@CENTUMBOOKSLTD.CO.UK

CENTUM BOOKS LIMITED REG. NO. 07641486

A CIP CATALOGUE RECORD FOR THIS BOOK IS AVAILABLE FROM THE BRITISH LIBRARY

PRINTED IN CHINA

ILLUMINATION PRESENTS

DESPICABLE ME3 ™

THE GREAT UNICORN QUEST

centum

STARRING . . .

AGNES: She loves unicorns, but she loves her family more.

MARGO: Agnes' oldest sister who's going through a 'teenage stage'.

EDITH: Goes on a quest with Agnes to find a unicorn (even though she doesn't believe they exist!).

LUCY: Agnes' mum, a spy for the AVL.

GRU: Agnes' dad, a former villain-turned-spy.

2 o o o o o o

DRU: Agnes' (new) uncle; her dad's identical twin.

9

WHAT IS A UNICORN?

If you LOVE unicorns as much as Agnes does, you'll be on the look-out for one at ALL TIMES.

THE HOOF PRINTS A UNICORN LEAVES BEHIND SPARKLE

UNICORNS LOVE TO PLAY NEAR RAINBOWS

UNICORNS LOVE TO EAT SWEETS AND CHOCOLATE

THEY LIVE IN FORESTS

Make sure you're always keeping your eyes open in case you spot any of the following 'unicorn' clues.**

BUTTERFLIES FOLLOW UNICORNS AROUND

THEY HAVE **LOVELY**, FLUFFY MANES AND TAILS

UNICORNS ARE **VERY** CUTE

THEY HAVE ONE MAGICAL HORN ON THEIR HEAD

** YOU'LL ONLY BE ABLE TO SPOT THESE CLUES IF YOU HAVE A PURE HEART.

Once upon a time, there was a little girl named AGNES. She had two older sisters – the eldest was called MARGO and the other was called EDITH. The three sisters were orphans and lived at 'Miss Hattie's Home for Girls'.

MISS HATTIE'S HOME FOR GIRLS

Edith
(THE MIDDLE SISTER)

Pink hat

Every night, when the girls went to sleep, **AGNES DREAMT THAT A MUMMY AND DADDY WOULD ADOPT THEM.** She was sure they would be adopted very soon and that the mummy and daddy would be nice . . .

Margo, Edith AND Agnes' ROOM IS HERE

EDITH IS PRAYING THAT BUGS DON'T CRAWL INTO THEIR BRAINS. GROSS!

. . . and have a pet
UNICORN.

AGNES **LOVED**
UNICORNS. ☺

She knew they were real. Every night she sang herself to
sleep with a song she had made up, all about unicorns.

AGNES' SONG

"Unicorns, I love them! Unicorns, I love them!

Uni, uni, unicorns, I lo-o-ove them!

Uni, unicorns, I could pet one, if they were

really real . . . and THEY ARE!

So, I bought one so I could pet it.

Now it loves me, now I love it!"

After she sang this, she always had the
MOST MAGICAL DREAMS all about unicorns.

AGNES'
TOY UNICORN

just not exactly as she had always imagined.

Agnes and her sisters were adopted by **Gru**, who was a "dentist".

Gru (NOT A DENTIST)

THE GIRLS FIRST MEET GRU

AGNES HAS GRU'S LEG

One day, Gru took the girls to 'SUPER SILLY FUN LAND' – the most fun place on Earth! It was here that Agnes first spotted something . . . FLUFFY.

It was **LOVE AT FIRST SIGHT!** The game they were playing was unfair, but luckily Gru had a gadget that helped to level the playing field...!

GRU'S GADGET WHICH LEVELS THE PLAYING FIELD!

From that moment on, Agnes and Fluffy did **EVERYONE** together.

FLUFFY IS **HERE!**

Tea parties with Gru, **stories at bedtime** . . .

ONE BIG UNICORN BY GRU

THIS STORY IS ABOUT UNICORNS TOO!

. . . and **board games** with Margo. They also slept together side-by-side every night. Agnes **LOVED** Fluffy **VERY MUCH.**

One very scary time, when the Minion Kevin was injected with PX-41, **PURPLE-KEVIN TRIED TO EAT FLUFFY!** Agnes **SCREAMED** so loudly that all the windows and Kevin's goggles shattered. Kevin dropped Fluffy. Agnes saved the day!

KEVIN'S GOGGLES **BEFORE** THEY WERE BROKEN!

NO ONE CAN COME BETWEEN A GIRL AND HER FLUFFY UNICORN!

As much as Agnes **LOVED** Fluffy, she loved
her family even more. So when her mummy
and daddy, Gru and Lucy, lost their jobs at
the AVL, Agnes knew what she had to do. She
held a yard sale to sell all her toys

- INCLUDING HER BELOVED FLUFFY.

FLUFFY BEING SOLD ☹

When the family went to visit Gru's new-found twin brother, Dru, in Freedonia, Agnes heard about a **LOCAL LEGEND**. The Legend stated that **REAL UNICORNS** roamed the nearby forest, and that if you were a maiden of the purest heart, you could find one.

AGNES AND EDITH EVEN FOUND A REAL UNICORN HORN IN A PUB! **PROOF!**

Agnes knew she had a **PURE HEART** so she knew just what she had to do . . .

Agnes and Edith set off into the forest, **DETERMINED** to find a **MYSTICAL UNICORN.**
It would fulfil Agnes' lifelong dream to find and become friends with a unicorn, and Edith's more recent dream (in case unicorns did exist) of filming a unicorn and selling the video to become rich.

THIS IS HOW EDITH FEELS ABOUT THE QUEST.

THIS IS HOW EDITH IMAGINES SHE'LL FEEL IF UNICORNS ARE REAL AND SHE FILMS IT.

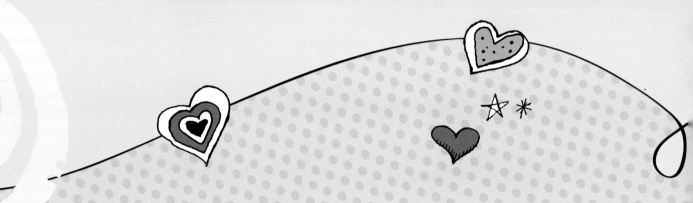

In the end, the maiden with the purest heart did find something that she knew was a unicorn in the forest.

AND iT WAS LOVE AT FiRST SiGHT.

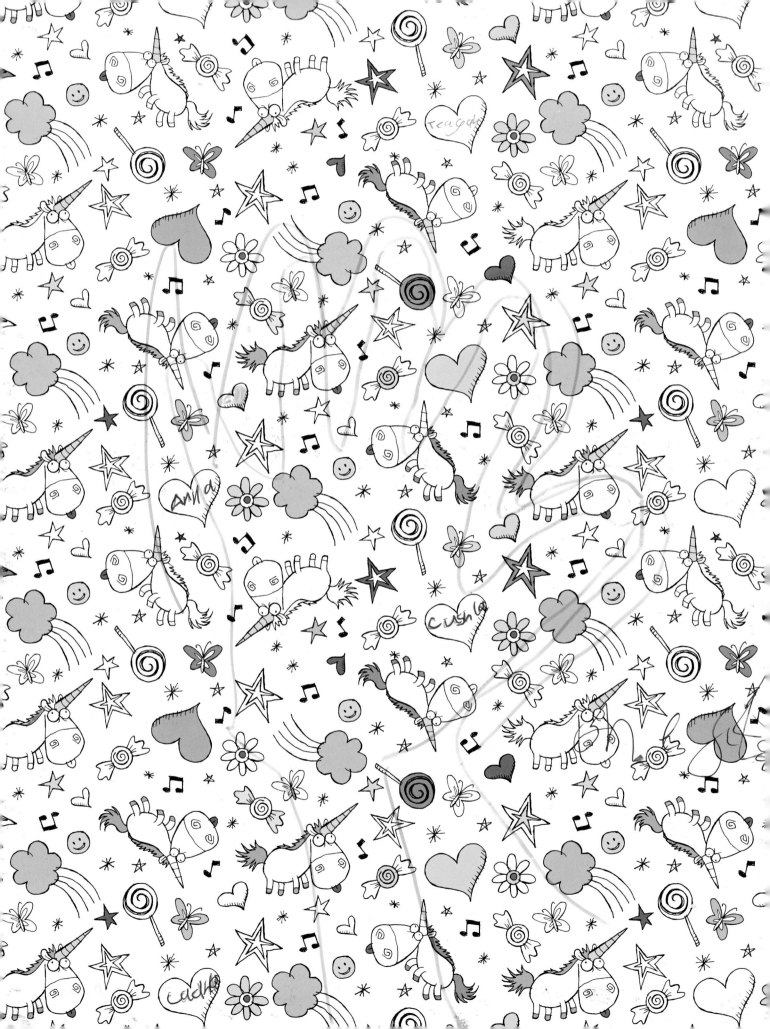